First published by Parragon in 2010

Parragon
Queen Street House
4 Queen Street
Bath BA1 1HE, UK

www.chuggington.com

© Ludorum plc 2009

ISBN 978-1-4454-1180-4

Printed in China

WAKE UP WILSON!

Based on the episode "Wake up Wilson!",
written by Ian Carney.

Bath · New York · Singapore · Hong Kong · Cologne · Delhi · Melbourne

ZOOOOOM!

One evening, Wilson and Koko were chasing each other around the park.

"Can't catch me!" shouted Wilson, laughing.

"Here I come, slow coach," Koko replied, zooming after him.

"YOU NEED AN EARLY NIGHT, WILSON. YOU HAVE YOUR FIRST MAIL RUN TOMORROW."

Vee said it was time for the trainees to go to bed. But Wilson wanted to have fun with Koko – he had forgotten all about the mail run!

At the roundhouses, Koko and Wilson dared each other to stay awake.

They lasted as long as they could, then Wilson heard Koko snoring.

"WAHAY, I WON,"

whispered Wilson, before falling asleep too.

In the morning, Wilson chugged sleepily towards the rolling stock yard and coupled up to a mail car.

YAWN!

"You've practised with this mail car lots of times before," said Dunbar, and reminded him what to do.

YAWN!

By the time Wilson reached the second station stop, he felt really sleepy.

Oil Can Eddie spotted Wilson from the track above. "Watch out, Wilson, your door's open mate," he said. Yawning, Wilson thanked Eddie and drove into the tunnel.

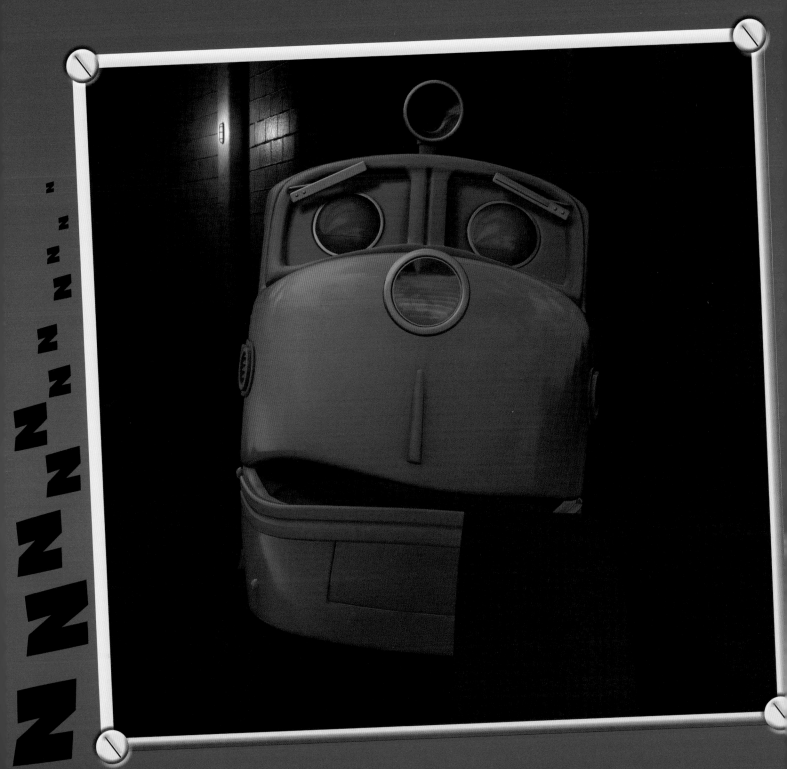

Wilson felt even sleepier inside the tunnel. It was dark and cosy, just like his roundhouse. He pulled over to the side of the track and fell asleep.

Meanwhile, Vee was looking for Wilson. He was supposed to be at the sorting office by noon.

WILSON, WHERE ARE YOU?....

Wilson woke up
and rolled out of
the tunnel.
"I'm here, Vee.
Don't worry, I'll
catch up," he
promised,
racing off.

Back at the depot, Koko overheard Dunbar and Vee talking about Wilson. They were worried he wouldn't make it to the sorting office on time.

"Oh, no! Wilson's tired 'cause I kept him up so late," thought Koko.

She raced off to see if she could help her sleepy friend.

CHOO CHOO!

HONK HONK!

Koko soon found Wilson who was asleep again at the side of the track. "Wake up, Wilson," cried Koko, sounding her horn.

Wilson woke up and gasped.

"Oh no! I've gotta shift my gears!"

At last, Wilson reached the sorting office with the Chuggington post. But the rest of the mail had already been taken to the branch stations.

The Chuggington post has never been late before.

Wilson felt terrible. It was all his fault.

Suddenly, he had an idea... he could sort the mail now and take it to all the branch stations himself. It would take a long time but the postmistress agreed to give it a try.

The mail was sorted into sacks, before being loaded into Wilson's car. Then Wilson dropped off a sack at each station.

At last, Wilson chugged into the depot. He'd done it! He had delivered all the Chuggington mail.

"I'm sorry I let you all down. It won't happen again," Wilson promised.

And it didn't! That night, Wilson had lots of sleep, and the next morning, he did the mail run on time.

CHUGGINGTON™

Complete your Chuggington collection.
Tick them off as you collect!

Stories
- CLUNKY WILSON — ISBN 978-1-4075-6041-0
- CAN'T CATCH KOKO — ISBN 978-1-4075-6042-7
- BRAKING BREWSTER — ISBN 978-1-4075-8009-8
- WAKE UP WILSON! — ISBN 978-1-4075-8010-4
- KOKO AND THE TUNNEL — ISBN 978-1-4075-9530-6
- BREWSTER GOES BANANAS — ISBN 978-1-4075-9531-3

Mini stories
- Braking Brewster — ISBN 978-1-4075-9331-9
- Clunky Wilson — ISBN 978-1-4075-9332-6
- Hodge and the Magnet — ISBN 978-1-4075-9333-3
- Koko and the Squirrels — ISBN 978-1-4075-9334-0
- Wilson Gets a Wash — ISBN 978-1-4075-9335-7
- Zephie's Zoom — ISBN 978-1-4075-9336-4

Activity books
- COPY COLOUR POSTER BOOK — ISBN 978-1-4075-6126-4
- STICKER SCENE STORY — ISBN 978-1-4075-6044-1
- Bumper Sticker Book — ISBN 978-1-4075-8141-5
- POSTER BOOK — ISBN 978-1-4075-9529-0
- ACTIVITY BOOK — ISBN 978-1-4075-9422-4
- My First Little Library — ISBN 978-1-4075-6043-4

Little library

Multi-play books
- Construct and Play! — ISBN 978-1-4075-9882-6
- Meet the Chuggers — ISBN 978-1-4075-9884-0

Annual
- CHUGGINGTON ANNUAL 2011 — ISBN 978-1-84535-437-4

Activity pack
- CHUGGER TRAVEL PACK — ISBN 978-1-4075-9885-7

3D books
- 3D — ISBN 978-1-4075-8349-5
- Chugger Sticker Colouring Pad — ISBN 978-1-4075-9780-5

Play books
- SING AND LEARN — ISBN 978-1-4075-6127-1
- KOKO ON CALL — ISBN 978-1-4075-8142-2

Story collection
- Storybook Collection — ISBN 978-1-4075-6046-5

Train books
- WILSON — LET'S RIDE THE RAILS! — ISBN 978-1-4075-8138-5
- KOKO — CHUGGA CHUGGA CHOO CHOO! — ISBN 978-1-4075-8139-2
- BREWSTER — HONKING HORNS! — ISBN 978-1-4075-8140-8